D'L

Mic

Mates

BY

Will Hanafin

Published in 2002 by
Merlin Publishing
16 Upper Pembroke Street
Dublin 2
Ireland
www.merlin-publishing.com

ISBN 1-903582-27-X

Typeset by Gough Typesetting Services, Dublin
Printed by Colour Books Ltd, Dublin

Contents

Mick's World

Ass If...

"I wasn't long training when I tore a stomach muscle which was a real pain in the ass."

Mick McCarthy • *Captain Fantastic*, O'Brien Press • 1990

Knee-capped For Ireland

"If that's a bad knee then I want two of them."

Mick McCarthy • RTÉ Radio 1 •
4 January 2002

Super Grans

"Not alone are the injured making speedy recoveries ahead of next month's friendly with Russia, but so are Irish grannies making miraculous appearances up and down Britain."

Mick McCarthy • *www.sports.com* •
13 January 2002

"Well, I've always said that if my granny was clean through I'd have kicked her, but I couldn't do that now could I – I'd get sent off."

Mick McCarthy • *Hot Press* •
29 November 1990

Legless!

"I think one or two of our legs got a bit leg-weary."

Mick McCarthy, Sky post-match analysis
Ireland v. Iran (Dublin) •
www.football365.com • 10 November
2001

Complete Zeros

"I played the last time in Seville, and we got beat 2-0, and to be honest we were lucky to get nil on the night."

Mick McCarthy • *Kenny Live*, RTÉ •
21 November 1992

Tummy Bug?

"For two days when I got the job I had a butterfly clumping around in my stomach with pit boots on – it worried me."

Mick McCarthy, on becoming Millwall manager • *RTÉ News* • 24 January 1993

The Second Coming

"Some didn't like me father, let's see how they get on with the son, eh."

Mick McCarthy, at press conference on becoming Irish manager • RTÉ • 1996

Well Matched

"People seem to think Jack and I are exactly the same, but I was a forthright, arrogant bastard before I ever got involved with him."

Mick McCarthy • *The Daily Telegraph* • 30 December 1996

Doubting Thomas

"When I have made up my mind about something and I am dead set on it, I would have to see the holes in the hands of anybody who wanted me to change my ideas."

Mick McCarthy • *The Mirror* • 29 October 1997

Mr. Motivator

"Well, I'm a motivator, if nothing else. If you watch the games you'll know I shout a lot. It might be a load of bollocks that I'm shouting but it's a funny thing about shouting a load of bollocks: it makes people respond, it gees them up."

Mick McCarthy • *Hot Press* •
29 November 1990

Baby Steps

"The thing is, I'm not quick, we all know that – I mean, I go out running and a woman with a pram passes me."

Mick McCarthy • *Hot Press* •
29 November 1990

Constructive Dismissal

"I told the chairman if he ever wants to sack me, all he has to do is to take me into town, buy me a meal and a few pints and a cigar and I'll piss off."

Mick McCarthy • *Sunday Tribune* •
6 April 1997

Little League

"We were forced to play so many youngsters that we had to burp and wind them after each game."

Mick McCarthy • *Sunday Tribune* • 6 April 1997

Heart Attackers

"But there have also been some pretty nifty small players who have made up for their lack of inches with big hearts."

Mick McCarthy • *The News of the World* • 29 August 1999

Girl Power

"Lady luck was playing midfield for us in the second half."

Mick McCarthy • *The Sunday Times* • 21 November 1999

Thick Skinned

"Having a neck like a jockey's whatsits certainly helps. As a player, I needed it, and, as a manager, I've needed it even more."

Mick McCarthy • *The Sun* • 11 October 2000

Would You Look At The Size Of That...

"Whatever provides a spark. I said to them have you seen the size of their lads."

Mick McCarthy after the Andorra game •
The Irish Times • 26 April 2001

Till Death Do You Part

"I do believe in partnerships on the football field and if your two centre-halves play well together... it might be important to keep that partnership and understanding."

Mick McCarthy • *The Soccer Show*, RTÉ • 19 March 1999

You Are Always On My Mind!

"I think I've only played about twelve games with somebody else and so, on the pitch, I've built up a strong bond with Kevin. It's that unseen, unwritten, unknown relationship that's just there; it's almost telepathic. And I think it's what partnerships are all about."

Mick McCarthy, on his relationship with Kevin Moran • *Hot Press* • 29 November 1990

Euroflash

"Foreign players are a bit cuter than our lads are, than the Irish, Scottish, English, Welsh lads."

Mick McCarthy • *Kenny Live*, RTÉ •
17 May 1997

Being Defensive

"I think you've gotta want to defend first and foremost. I think people overlook the fact defending is a skill."

Mick McCarthy, on being asked what makes a good defender • *The Grip*, RTÉ • 22 March 1996

Is There Any Other Way?

"If I want to tell somebody something, I walk up to him, I pick the phone up and I tell him – that's the way I do it."

Mick McCarthy, at the Roy Keane row press conference • *RTÉ Sport* • 29 May 1996

Dumbstruck

"I'm absolutely thrilled that I went to Busan... when our flag came out I had a lump in my throat, goose pimples all over and the hairs stood up on the back of my neck."

Mick McCarthy • *The Irish Mirror* • 3 December 2001

Team Effort

"I was knackered when I come off. I kicked every ball with the lads."

Mick McCarthy, after Republic of Ireland drew 1-1 with England • RTÉ • 28 March 1991

Home Advantage

"All the players have always thought we should have a home of our own. And that's not changed."

Mick McCarthy • *RTÉ News* • 6 April 2000

Tug Of War

"We could send them up the River Liffey on a tug boat or something but what's the point? I'm not into that stuff."

Mick McCarthy, on showing the Turkish team the sights before the Euro 2000 play-off • *The Irish Times* • 25 October 1999

'Allo, 'Allo

"Some lads I played against would scream blue murder and roll around on the ground in front of the referee if you even said bonjour to them."

Mick McCarthy • *Captain Fantastic,* O'Brien Press • 1990

On A Roll

"He went down like a role of lino"

Mick McCarthy, talking on BBC • quoted in *The Irish Times* • 4 February 2002

Monster Mix!

"A mix of Niall Quinn, Robbie Keane, Damien Duff, Frank Stapleton and Don Givens, who is qualified to play for Ireland."

Mick McCarthy's ideal player • *The Sunday Business Post* • 6 January 2002

Bird Brains!

*"Some of the lads had never had one,
others thought a curfew was a small
flightless bird with a long beak!"*

Mick McCarthy • *Captain Fantastic*,
O'Brien Press • 1990

Figuring Out The Opposition

"It is the team we will be playing against, not anything else."

Mick McCarthy • Euro 2000 website

Mick Who?

"Gullit is probably going around his dressingroom wanting to know who owns this Irish shirt?"

Mick McCarthy, on swapping jerseys with Ruud Gullit in Euro '88 • *Captain Fantastic*, O'Brien Press • 1990

A Lump In His Throat

"Some of you fellas maybe hyped it up that this game was going to be easy, and my colleague here (the Icelandic manager), who has swallowed the Blarney Stone, told us all week that they were missing players..."

Mick McCarthy, on drawing with Iceland in the World Cup 1998 qualifier • *The Irish Times* • 11 November 1996

Mick and the Players

He Doesn't Phone... He Doesn't Write!

"I've not heard from Phil. We've tried everywhere, bar contacting Interpol, but no one knows where he is."

Mick McCarthy, on looking for Phil Babb before Ireland's World Cup qualifier against Romania • *The Sunday Times* • 28 December 1997

Window Display

"I'm delighted for him, he epitomised the work ethic in my team. He was magnificent out there today and if that lad can't get another club then I'll display my backside in Burton's window."

Mick McCarthy, on Jason McAteer • *The Irish Times* • 3 September 2001

They Deserved To Win!

"In the end I was just happy that we didn't lose and I think it would have been an injustice if Denis (Irwin) had scored a second goal from that free-kick towards the end."

Mick McCarthy, on the 1-1 draw with Belgium on the first leg of the World Cup qualifying play-off • *The Mirror* • 3 November 1997

Hands Off!

"At the moment he's injured and I am not going to give him any little carrot to grab hold of. I think he's got to rehabilitate properly first for his own sake."

Mick McCarthy, on Keith O'Neill • *The Irish Times* • 18 October 1997

Which Team Are We, Mick?

"I don't think he had the best first-half but maybe the way we played confused him."

Mick McCarthy, on Lee Carsley after the Romanian game • *The Irish Times* • 18 October 1997

Keanomania

"I've said to Roy himself it's like having an icon, it's like having the Beatles in."

Vow Of Silence

"Everything he does and everything he says is highlighted and that's probably the reason why for years he didn't say anything."

Mick McCarthy, on Roy Keane • *The Irish Independent* • 10 November 2001

Vote Of No Confidence

"He repaid what little faith I showed in him."

Mick McCarthy, on Tony Cascarino after he scored two goals against Lithuania, securing Ireland's place in the World Cup play-offs • *The Mirror* • 15 September 1997

Under Lock And Key

"It was Andy who really turned it on under the Stamford Bridge lights. He spent the night shackling Dutchman Jimmy Floyd Hasselbaink."

Mick McCarthy, on Andy O'Brien • *Ireland on Sunday* • 16 December 2001

Mick's Mangled Clichés

Getting It Ass-ways

"My heart was pounding and I was feeling as sick as the proverbial donkey."

Mick McCarthy, after the 4-2 World Cup victory over Iceland • *The Independent* • 13 September 1997

Pyrrhic Victory?

"He was having a hard game against Ginola. I'll tell you what... he won the battle in the end. He lost a couple of the wars but he won the battle in the end."

Mick McCarthy, on Denis Irwin • *The Grip*, RTÉ • 22 March 1996

Handyman

"He's a jack of all trades but he's a master of them as well. He's good at them."

Mick McCarthy, on Roy Keane • *The Soccer Show*, RTÉ • 19 March 1999

Mick's Rants

Mad Hatter

"UEFA will think of some stupid way to draw it out. They won't just draw one out of the hat and then the next one will they? That will be far too easy. They'll do some hifalutin, new-fangled way of drawing it out and make a cock up of it like they normally do."

Mick McCarthy, on Euro 2000 draw • *The Irish Times* • 11 October 1999

Jumping On The Bandwagon?

"And if people want to jump on the Mick McCarthy's-a-great-guy bandwagon then let them jump on it; and if they all want to jump on the Mick McCarthy's-a-complete-dickhead bandwagon let them stay on it. It genuinely doesn't bother me."

Mick McCarthy • *The Observer* • 9 September 2001

Causing A Stink

"*Yeah we played well, we had a good team but didn't qualify. And do you know what? It would have hung around my neck like a bad smell.*"

Mick McCarthy • *The Sunday Independent* • 30 December 2001

You're Not Upset... By Any Chance?

"It was one of those things. The guy could play for a hundred years and never get the ball put on his forehead like that again. But do I ever watch it? Do I hell? Do I stick needles in my eyes? Do I put hot coals under me finger nails?"

Mick McCarthy, on *that* Macedonian goal
• *The Irish Times* • 17 March 2001

Quintessential Mick

"Anyone who uses the term 'quintessentially' in a speech is talking crap."

Mick McCarthy • *The Sunday Times* • 20 December 1998

It Just Doesn't Add Up

"Everything I seem to do is wrong. I go for 4-3-3 and it's wrong. I go for 4-4-2 and it's wrong, I go for 4-5-1 and it's wrong."

Mick McCarthy, quoted after Packie Bonner's testimonial • *The Sunday Times* • 28 December 1997

I'm Saying Nothing!

"I could come in after a game like that and say that it was bobbins, we didn't play well, we didn't get great crosses in, we could have scored more goals, we were pure *****. I could say that, but I'm not going to."

Mick McCarthy, after the Andorra game • *The Irish Times* • 30 April 2001

Poetic Justice

"We're football people, not poets, but obviously I'm disappointed with the result."

Mick McCarthy • *The Sunday Mail* • 31 December 2000

Coffee Mourning

"I lashed the coffee mugs around. I'm sure they'll be sending me a bill cos I booted one and me foot was stuck up the fucking thing for about 15 minutes I think."

Mick McCarthy, after Belgium play-off • *McCarthy's Park*, RTÉ • 2 February 1998

Mugshots

"Whoever we play won't be mugs, they'll be good, well organised football teams.

Mick McCarthy • *The Irish Times* • 8 October 2001

A Forgettable Performance

"FIFA stands for Forget Irish Football Altogether."

Mick McCarthy • *Saturday Live*, RTÉ •
27 November 1999

The Commentators

Strange Fruit

*"Well they're glum oranges aren't they?
I'd say the fruit most akin to the flavour
they're feeling at the moment is the
lemon."*

George Hamilton, Ireland v. Holland •
RTÉ Sport • 1 September 2001

Fair Weather Supporter

"Cyprus with the wind in their faces in the second-half. Judging where the trajectory of the aircraft leaving Collinstown International (Airport) – I'd say the wind is south-easterly."

George Hamilton lets his gaze wander skywards during Cyprus v. Ireland • *RTÉ Sport* • 6 October 2001

Pull Yourselves Together!

"There hasn't been as much shape to Ireland that there was in the first-half. The wide men haven't gone wide – to the same extent in this early phase of the second."

George Hamilton, Ireland v. Cyprus • *RTÉ Sport* • 6 October 2001

Getting It In The Neck

"If we lose I will hang myself from the crossbar – I hope you will grieve for me."

Miroslav Blazevic, Iranian Coach • *The Irish Times* • 12 November 2001

Aerial Threat

"At one stage I found myself discussing flight paths that would not avoid missile paths."

FAI boss Bernard O'Byrne, after talks with UEFA about travelling to Macedonia • *The Mirror* • 26 March 1999

He's Right Behind You!

"I have great respect for their manager Mick McCarthy because he is one of the top managers in the world if you look at his record. But in the time I have known him his hair has turned white – and he frightens me."

Iranian coach Blazevic again • *The Irish Times* • 12 November 2001

Out Of This World

"I don't like to see teams of this calibre in World Cup football; I think they belong elsewhere."

Begrudging Acceptance

"Sometimes you have got to accept a goal on its virtues, even if it is scored by one of the world's most obscure sides."

Mark Lawrenson, on the extra-terrestrial Andorrans • *The Irish Times* • 26 April 2001

Outside The Eurozone

"We probably got on better with the likes of Holland, Belgium, Norway and Sweden, some of whom are not even European."

Jack Charlton • *The Sunday Mail* • 31 December 2000

UN Ambassador

"The Spaniards and the Danes will be crapping themselves when they hear our result. I don't mind the Danes but I can't stand Spain."

Jack Charlton • *The Daily Telegraph* • 19 June 1993

Covering All The Options

"If in winning we only draw we would be fine."

Jack Charlton • *The Sunday Mail* •
31 December 2000

"It was a game we should have won. We lost it because we thought we were going to win it. But then again, I thought that there was no way we were going to get a result there."

Jack Charlton, on the Romanian game •
The Sunday Mail • 31 December 2000

A Fertile Imagination

"My advice to Roy Keane is to ignore the thought that the grass is greener elsewhere because he might find the cows have crapped on it."

Brian Clough advises Roy to stay put at Manchester United • *The Sunday Mail* • 31 December 2000

Pointing Fingers

"If the fourth official had done his job correctly it wouldn't have happened... but I don't want to blame anyone."

John Aldridge as Tranmere Boss • *The Sunday Mail* • 31 December 2000

Green With Envy

"It was lovely and green."

Roy Keane, asked by a Dutch journalist about the state of the Lansdowne Road pitch • *The Irish Times* • 3 September 2001

Latvia?

"All you can say about the Estonians is that they were spirited but if they'd played any deeper they'd have been in the next country."

Mark Lawrenson • *The Irish Times* •
7 June 2001

You Are The Weakest Link!

"But we all know that any team is only as strong as its weakest link and that's been our strength throughout – there hasn't been a weak link."

Mark Lawrenson • *The Irish Times* • 16 November 2001

Eamon Dunphy

Final Answer?

"I didn't think McCarthy could sink any lower in my estimation, but this is the stupidest team selection imaginable."

Eamon Dunphy, on team selection against Romania • *The Sunday Times* • 28 December 1997

Final Answer?

"Asked how long Irish fans would have to wait before we once again had an active interest in the World Cup, Dunphy said: 'After Mick McCarthy has departed. And you can quote me on that.'"

The Irish Mirror • 8 June 1998

Final Answer!

"*Right now, Mick McCarthy has done a magnificent job as manager of the Irish team... of this squad of players.*"

Eamon Dunphy • *RTÉ News* •
9 November 2001

Mick's Mates

Funny That!

"*Their anthem sounds a bit funny but the crowd knows every word and join in.*

Jason McAteer, on Iran v. Ireland in Tehran • *Sunday Independent* • 18 November 2001

Room With A View

"I think at the end of the day our dressing room was more disappointed than theirs."

Kevin Sheedy • *RTÉ Sport* • 28 March 1991

Below the Belt

"It was a kick in the privates."

Gary Kelly, on losing 1-0 to Croatia • *The Irish Times* • 6 September 1999

Ouch!

"In the first-half they were playing long balls to the flanks but in the second-half they changed that and we had to deal with it."

Ian Harte • *The Irish Mirror* • 16 November 2001

Outnumbered

"It's difficult to play any sort of penetrating football when you're up against a side that is determined to keep 11 men behind the ball from beginning to end."

Matt Holland • *The Irish Times* • 29 March 2001

Figure Head

"I've given up on the club and it's best they let me go without putting a ridiculous figure on my head."

Mark Kennedy, on troubles at Liverpool • *The Mirror* • 3 November 1997

Extra Time!

"I spent a month in Ireland one week."

Mick McCarthy • *McCarthy's Park*, RTÉ • 2
February 1998